RABBIT & BEAR

Attack of the Snack

STORY BY
JULIAN GOUGH

ILLUSTRATIONS BY
JIM FIELD

Silver Dolphin

Silver Dolphin Books
An imprint of Printers Row Publishing Group
A division of Readerlink Distribution Services, LLC
10350 Barnes Canyon Road, Suite 100, San Diego, CA 92121
www.silverdolphinbooks.com

All notations of errors or omissions should be addressed to
Silver Dolphin Books, Editorial Department, at the above address. All other correspondence
(author inquiries, permissions) concerning the content of this book should be addressed to:
Hodder Children's Books, Carmelite House, 50 Victoria Embankment, London, EC4Y 0DZ

Library of Congress Cataloging-in-Publication Data

Names: Gough, Julian, author. | Field, Jim, 1980- illustrator.
Title: Rabbit & Bear: attack of the snack / story by Julian Gough ;
illustrations by Jim Field. Other titles: Rabbit and Bear, attack of the snack
Description: San Diego, CA : Silver Dolphin, an imprint of Printers Row
Publishing Group, [2020] | Audience: Ages 6-8. | Audience: Grades 2-3. |
Summary: When Rabbit and Bear's swim is disturbed by a small owl,
Bear is interested in learning more but Rabbit relates horror stories and
wants to imprison the sleeping bird.
Identifiers: LCCN 2019030324 | ISBN 9781684126170 (hardcover) | ISBN 9781645171744 (ebook)
Subjects: CYAC: Individuality--Fiction. | Friendship--Fiction. | Rabbits--Fiction. | Bears--Fiction. |
Animals--Fiction. | Humorous stories. Classification: LCC PZ7.1.G6863 Rab 2019 | DDC [E]--dc23
LC record available at https://lccn.loc.gov/2019030324

ISBN: 978-1-68412-617-0
Manufactured, printed, and assembled in Dongguan, China.
First printing, December 2019. RRD/12/19
23 22 21 20 19 1 2 3 4 5

For Sandy, always

J.F.

●

To my friend Neil Farrell, whom I first met under a table when we were schoolchildren. What a great day! (He was reciting Monty Python sketches, brilliantly; and I was enchanted.) And to his wonderful mother, Una Farrell, who took me in, and fed me, and gave me a key to their Galway home (and let me sleep there for months), at a time in my life when I was particularly bedraggled, having been chased out of the next valley by killer burping owls.

J.G.

THREE SISTER MOUNTAINS

THE CLIFF OF A
THOUSAND BIRDS

BEAR'S CAVE

WOODPECKER'S
TREE

RABBIT'S
WARREN

GIANT
SANDPIT

THE
FLOWER
CLEARING

One summer's day, Rabbit and Bear were swimming in the lake.

"This," said Rabbit, "is the Best Day Ever."

Then a Thing whizzed over their heads.

The Thing screamed, hit a tree, and fell
into the water.

SPLASH!

Wooo ooo OOO ooo OOO!!!

"How VERY interesting," said Bear.

"Aaargh! URRGH! Horrible!" said Rabbit.

"I wonder what that was?" said Bear.

"*That* was the most hideous Thing in the world," said Rabbit, "and *this* is the Worst Day Ever."

The Thing popped back up.

Rabbit grabbed Bear's chin, and pulled.

"If I could just..." said Rabbit, "...use your face...as a ladder..."

Rabbit climbed up
Bear's face, and sat on
her head. Safe!

"Thanks," said Rabbit.

Bear lifted the soggy
Thing out of the water.

"Do you know what
this is, Rabbit?"

"Of *course* I do," said
Rabbit. "It's a..."

Rabbit scratched his head.

"It's a…"

Rabbit scratched his butt.

"It's a…"

OK, better say *something*!

"It's a Trumpwig! A Taxbill! A Wetfart!"

"It's a *what*?" said Bear.

"OK, OK, I *don't* know," said Rabbit. "I just made up the scariest words I could think of."

Bear carried the Mysterious Thing ashore. She tipped it upside down until water fell out of it. The Thing gave a little cough. And then a little sigh. And then a little snore.

"A Thing, with feathers..." said
Bear. "Is it a bird?"

"Maybe it's one of Woodpecker's cousins, from the next valley," said Rabbit.

Bear rolled the Thing over.

"Wow!" said Rabbit. "It hit the tree so hard, its face went *flat*!"

"Let's take her to Woodpecker," said Bear.

9

They followed the noise of
Woodpecker wood-pecking, until
they got to the giant sandpit.

BANG!
BANG!
BANG!

"Yum! Yum! Yum!"

Woodpecker was in a hollow tree stump, eating delicious grubs.

"Hey Woodpecker," said Rabbit. "Your cousin banged her face flat."

Woodpecker flew down to look.

"That's not a wood-wood-woodpecker!" she said. "I think it's an ow-ow-owl! My grandmother told me they've got flat-flat-flat faces!"

"An owl!!!" said Rabbit. "Owls are *dangerous*!" He jumped backwards, away from the small, soggy owl, and landed in some stinging nettles.

OW! MY BUTT!

He jumped sideways, and
landed upside down in some spiky
brambles. *"See?"* said Rabbit. "See
how dangerous owls are?"

"I've never seen an owl before," said Bear.

"Ex! Ex! Exciting!" said Woodpecker.

"*Exciting?!* It's terrifying!" said Rabbit. "My grandfather told me all about owls!" Rabbit pointed at the tiny, sleeping owl. "Owls are six feet tall! With claws like swords! And they eat you ALIVE! And the next day, they BURP UP YOUR BONES!"

"One bone at a time, or all of them at once?" asked Bear, interested.

"All at once!" said Rabbit. "Burped up in a neat little package, wrapped in YOUR OWN SKIN, like a birthday present MADE OUT OF YOU!"

16

"No! No! No!" said Woodpecker. "My grand-grand-grandmother told me owls are incredibly wise and clean and kind-kind-kind and smart-smart-smart and smell like mint."

SNIFF

"Nonsense!" said Rabbit.

Bear sniffed the owl. "I don't smell
any mint."

"The only thing this owl smells like is BEING HORRIBLE," said Rabbit.

"Um..." said Bear, "have either of you ever *met* an actual owl?"

"Of course I, er...haven't," said Rabbit.

"Not an Ak! Ak! Actual owl..." said Woodpecker.

"But that is not the point!" said Rabbit and Woodpecker together. "I know *exactly* what owls are like!"

"Wise and Wonderful!" said Woodpecker.

"HURTFUL and HORRIBLE!" said Rabbit.

He shouted this so loudly, Woodpecker fell over backwards.

"Hey! Hey! Hey!" said Woodpecker. "That's rude-rude-rude!"

And she flew away.

"Hah!" said Rabbit.

"I won the argument!

With my brilliant ideas!"

"I don't think you won the argument," said Bear doubtfully. "I think you just shouted the loudest."

"SAME THING!" shouted Rabbit. Wow, shouting was fun.

"I AM THE WINNER!"

He shouted so loudly that other animals started running towards the sandpit to see what was happening. Except Mole, who started digging.

"So what did you win?" asked Mouse, and poked Owl in the tummy so hard that the sleeping owl farted.

"Oh no! It's a Wetfart!" said Vole.

"WORSE!" said Rabbit. "It's...an owl! A seven-foot-tall burping killer!"

The other animals looked
at the tiny, snoring owl and
gasped.

Then they looked again.

"It looks...small," said Mole.

"And damp," said Mouse
in her squeaky voice.

"Did she kill *you*, Rabbit?" asked Vole, nervously. "With a giant burp?"

"Worse!" said Rabbit. "She threw me into the nettles! Look!" And Rabbit showed them his stung butt.

"Ugh!" "Awk!" "Horrible!" said the other animals, and covered their eyes.

"Oh, *bad* owl!" said Vole.

26

"Er, Rabbit, that's not really what happened," said Bear, but the other animals were too excited to listen.

Mole was getting grumpy in the blazing sunshine. "We must do something about this owl!" he said. "She is making me too hot!"

"Tickle her hard!" shouted Mouse.

"Tell her she is naughty! In a big angry voice!" shouted Vole.

"No!" said Rabbit. "Even better! Throw the terrible owl in prison before she wakes up, eats us, burps up our bones, and uses them to decorate her home for Halloween!"

"Yes!" said Mole and Mouse and Vole. "Throw her in prison! Hooray!"

There was a pause.

"What's a prizzin?" said Vole.

"A prison is a place where you can lock up EIGHT-FEET-TALL KILLER BURPING OWLS," said Rabbit.

"Hooray!" cheered the animals.

All except Bear.

Bear leaned over and whispered to Rabbit, "Wouldn't it be *fairer* to wait until the owl wakes up? And then talk to her? She might be...nice."

"You are being very reasonable. And sensible. And calm," said Rabbit to Bear.

"Oh, thank you," said Bear, relieved.

"Stop it at once!" said Rabbit fiercely. "I am protecting the valley, and keeping us safe! Go away if you won't help."

Bear sighed. She didn't want to fight with Rabbit. Over Rabbit's shoulder, Bear spotted some blueberry bushes. And mint. "Well, I suppose I do need breakfast."

Bear wandered off.

"Now what?" said the other animals.

Rabbit hopped up onto the hollow tree stump.

"I accuse this nine-foot-tall owl of stinging butts with nettles!" shouted Rabbit.

"Boooo!" shouted Mole and Mouse and Vole. "Bad Owl!"

"I accuse this owl," shouted Rabbit, "of... of...of millions of crimes against rabbits and mice and moles and voles and plants and ants and trees and bees and land and sand and...!"

"Boooo!"

"I accuse this owl..." Rabbit paused dramatically, and the animals all held their breath, "...of being an OWL!!!" said Rabbit.

"BOOOO!" said all the animals. "Worst crime ever!"

The tiny owl snored, and rolled over in her sleep.

"Throw this wicked owl in prison!" cried Rabbit.

Everybody started cheering, then stopped.

"We don't have a prizzin," said Vole.

Mouse pointed at Owl, and shouted, "I accuse you of...not building a prison!"

"Booooooo!" shouted the animals. "Crimiest crime ever!"

"I have an idea!" said Mole.
"We can put Owl...in the
hollow tree stump!"

"Hooray!"

And all the little animals
rolled the small, wet,
sleeping owl into the hollow
tree stump.

"Lock her up!"

Mole and Vole jammed sticks into the soft wood.

Rabbit and Mouse wrapped the tree in spiky brambles.

"Hooray!"
the animals shouted.
"The wicked owl is
in prison!"

"Bad, bad Owl!" said Vole, and threw a blueberry at Owl.

It bounced off her tummy.

Owl opened one eye.

"The prisoner is waking up!" said Mouse.

Owl opened the other eye.

The animals gasped and stepped back.

Owl picked up the
blueberry, and ate it.

Then she shook the water
out of her feathers, until
she looked like a bird again.

"Hmmm," said Bear,
wandering back. "That's a
funny-looking house."

"Whoooo...Whoooo...Whoooo used my head as a bongo drum?" said Owl, feeling the bump on her head.

"You hit your head on a tree," said Bear, still munching berries.

"Oh yes," said Owl. "I was flying tooooooo...tooooooo...tooooo fast...Am I dead?" She looked around her, at the inside of the rotten tree. "If this is Heaven...I'm *very* disappointed."

"No," said Rabbit importantly, "you are in prison."

"Oh dear," said Bear. She shouldn't have left Rabbit in charge...

"In PRISON?" said Owl. "Did I commit a crime in my SLEEP?"

"Um," said Mouse.

"What did I doooooo...dooooo...dooooo wrong?"

"Er..." said Mole, and looked down and shuffled his paws.

"She doesn't LOOK like a nine-foot-tall burping killer," whispered Vole.

"Did I drop litter?" said Owl. "I can pick it up."

"No," said Mole, "we just thought...you might kill us, and, you know, eat us, and um...burp up our bones."

"Wait," said Bear. "All of you put this little owl in prison because you thought she might *eat* someone in the *future*?"

"Yes," said Vole.

"You think I'm a hungry, time-travelling criminal?!" said Owl.

"No..." Mouse felt strangely embarrassed.

"So why am I in prison?"

Rabbit was starting to feel like he had made a terrible mistake. He didn't like the feeling.

"How much do you know about owls?" said Owl.

"Er..." said Mole.

"Owls are ten feet tall!" shouted Rabbit, but now shouting didn't make him feel better. It made him feel worse.

A little voice, deep inside him, said, what if you are *wrong*?

"THEY'RE KILLERS!" Rabbit shouted, even louder, to silence the little voice. "WHO BURP!"

"Well, OK, true, horned owls are big, and eat rabbits," said the little owl. "And eagle owls—big. Fish owls are very big. And the great gray owl is very, very big. *Their* wings can stretch five feet wide."

The animals
gasped, and stepped
backwards until they
bumped into Bear.

Bear's tummy full of
blueberries rumbled.

"But I'm not that
kind of owl," said Owl.

MoooOOOOooooo

"Don't listen to the eleven-foot-tall killer!" shouted Rabbit, and he shut his eyes, to check the pictures in his head. Yes, owls were big and mean and...and...and... HORRIBLE! "They're all the same!"

"No, we're *not*," said Owl. "There are teeny, tiny owls tooooo, tooooo, tooooo. Elf owls! Pygmy owls! And *me*. I'm pretty much the smallest owl there is. And I eat *fruit* and *insects*. Come here and see, you big, mean rabbit."

Me, *big*? Me, *mean*? Rabbit opened his eyes, put up his fists, and walked very, VERY slowly up to the prison bars.

Owl raised her wing, and pushed it out between the bars and the brambles, until it just reached Rabbit's nose.

"See? Yooooou... yooooooou...yoooooou *are* bigger than me."

"Oh, your feathers are *soft*," said Rabbit, dropping his fists. "I thought they would be hard, and sharp as knives."

Bear sighed. "Just let Owl out of prison, Rabbit. You made a mistake, that's all. It's OK."

"No, it's not!" said Rabbit. His next thought was more scary than a giant killer burping owl snacking on an elephant.

"If I made a mistake…then I'm not *perfect*. And you won't like me any more."

"What?" said Bear. "It's exactly the opposite, Rabbit! NOBODY is perfect, EVER. We *all* make mistakes. We *have to*! It's how we learn!"

"YOU don't make mistakes, Bear," said Rabbit.

"Yes I do! I just made one! I should have stopped you being so silly with Owl earlier, but I didn't want to argue with my friend." Bear's tummy rumbled again. "AND I just made the mistake of eating too many blueberries...look, just let Owl go."

"But..." said Rabbit. "What if she's a horrible giant killer burping owl? They ARE real!"

"They may be real IN SOME
OTHER VALLEY," said Bear.
"But here and now, they are just
an idea in your head. Look at
the *real* owl in *front* of you."

Rabbit looked.

She was small. And friendly.

Nothing like the idea in his head.

63

Oh *dear*, thought Rabbit. Why did I
put this lovely little owl in prison?
Maybe Bear was right.

"I..." said Rabbit, "made a..."

Whew, it was very hard to say it. It felt like coughing up a rock.

"...mistake."

Oh, wow. It WAS like coughing up a rock! A huge weight had left Rabbit!

SORRY?

An even bigger weight lifted off Rabbit! He felt lighter than air! He had to check that his feet were still on the ground.

"I'm really sorry!" said Rabbit, bouncing up and down with lightness and gladness. "I'm not just saying it! I actually mean it!"

He unwrapped the brambles.

Owl stepped out, and shook her feathers.

"I'm sorry I threw a blueberry at you," said Vole.

"That's OK," said Owl. "It was delicious."

"I'm sorry I poked your tummy," said Mouse.

"That's OK," said Owl. "I like tickles."

Rabbit remembered something else.
"WOODPECKER! I'M SORRY I
SHOUTED AT YOU!" shouted Rabbit.
Woodpecker flew back.
"That's OK," said
Woodpecker. "I Flew!
Flew! Flew! Into your
burrow, and pooped all
over your favorite chair,
and now I feel MUCH
better."
"Gah!" said Rabbit.

Bear sighed. "Woodpecker..."

"OK, OK, OK, I'm sorry-sorry-sorry!" said Woodpecker.

Everyone said sorry to everyone else, until they were friends again.

SORRY!

SORRY SORRY SORRY

"Owl," said Rabbit.

"Can we *help* you?"

"Well..." said Owl, "I don't have anywhere tooooo tooooo tooooo live...Could you help me build a new home?"

"Oh...I'd love to," said Rabbit. "But...I can't climb trees." He sighed.

Owl laughed. "You don't know ANYTHING about owls like me! Watch..."

And she started digging
into the soft, sandy ground.
In a few seconds she had
disappeared.

"Wow!" said Rabbit.

Owl popped back up.
"I'm a burrowing owl!"

"Oh, I can help you with
that!" said Rabbit.

"I'll help too!" said Mole.

They started burrowing.

"This sand is much nicer for digging than my old rocky island," said Owl, as they dug together.

"And there are no big, mean, killer burping owls to chase me, and try to eat me..."

"Big owls eat *little* owls?" said Mole.

"Yes! We're their *snacks*! That's why I was flying so fast!"

"They chased you all the way here?" said Vole. "From the next valley?"

"Yes. Because I made a joke about them." Owl sighed. "And killer burping owls just don't have a sense of humor."

"I have a sense of humor!" shouted Vole, excited.

Vole had only discovered she had a sense of humor the day before, when Bear had farted a tune by mistake, and Vole had laughed for three hours. Vole was very keen to use her sense of humor again.

"Can you *fart* any jokes?" said Vole.

"I could try," said Owl. "But I'm better at burps."

"Burps are good, too," said Vole, generously.

"Wouldn't it be nice," said Mouse, "if we had a place just to make each other laugh…"

"We can turn the prison into a stage!" said Vole. "For jokes!"

"A lovely idea," said Bear.

Mouse and Vole pulled down all the sticks and brambles. They built a ladder from the sticks, and made the stump into a summer stage.

Bear made daisy chains and hung them around the edge.

"Thunder!" said Rabbit, looking up.

GRRRuuuMMBLE!

"No, it's my tummy," said Bear. "Er, I need to do...something. In the woods. Excuse me."

Bear trotted off.

At last Rabbit
said, "Whew,
your new home is
finished."

"Almost." Owl
looked around.

"I just need *one more thing,*" she said.

At that moment, Bear came back.

Owl sniffed, in the direction Bear had come from. "What a great smell! It's exactly what I need to make my new home perfect..."

And Owl ran into the woods.

"Oh dear," said Bear.

Owl came back rolling an enormous ball of Bear's poop.

"This is perfect!" Owl said. "Blueberry poop!"

"What," said Rabbit, "...will you do...with that blueberry poop?"

"Cover the walls of my burrow with it, of course," said Owl politely.

"You use *poop* as *wallpaper*!?" said Rabbit and Bear and Woodpecker and Mole and Mouse and Vole.

"Oh yes. It's what burrowing owls doooooo...doooooo...doooooo. We love pooooooo...pooooooo...pooooooo...Don't yoooooooou...yoooooooou...yoooooooou?"

"Let's not talk about that," said Rabbit, who had some very unusual poop habits of his own. "WHY POOP WALLPAPER?"

"To attract delicious, crunchy dung beetles, of course," said Owl. "They *love* the smell of poop..."

"You eat DUNG BEETLES?" said Mole, as he chewed on a delicious, wriggly worm. "UGH!"

Woodpecker stopped licking delicious wriggly grubs with her spiky tongue. "DUNG BEETLES?" she said. "ICKY! BLECHY! YUCKY!"

"Well...there are worse things you could eat," said Rabbit, who ate worse things every morning.

A shiny dung beetle ran towards the enormous ball of poop.

"See?" Owl picked it up and ate it. "Delicious! Crunchy! Snacks!"

"Your food *delivers itself*?" said Rabbit.

"From miles around!" said Owl. "Fast foooooo…fooooooo…foooooood!"

Another dung beetle ran by.

"VERY fast!" Owl ate it. "They're delicious with mint." She plucked a few leaves and ate them.

"Oh, I love you, Owl," said Rabbit, and stuck his head down Owl's tunnel to admire the wallpaper.

"I've never met anyone who has worse habits than me."

"Thank you!" said Owl.

"We all look normal on the outside, Rabbit," said Bear. "But, just like our burrows, and caves, and tunnels, and nests..."

"We're weird on the inside!" said Rabbit.

"Yes," said Bear. She smiled. "And that's OK."